A TEAM DIVIDED

By Tracey West

SCHOLASTIC INC.

ISBN 978-0-545-74640-3

12 11 10 9 8 7 6 5 4 3 2 1   15 16 17 18 19 20/0

Printed in the U.S.A.   40
First printing, January 2015

CONTENTS

FROM THE JOURNAL OF

Sensei Garmadon

injago™ is still recovering from the assault by the Digital Overlord. His dark spirit infested cyberspace, seeking a way to steal my son, Lloyd's, Golden Power so he could become the Golden Master. And he succeeded.

It looked as though all was lost. In the Serpentine legend, the Golden Master was called the Destroyer. Unless someone stopped him, nothing would survive.

Then one brave ninja made the ultimate sacrifice to defeat the Golden Master: Zane.

Using his mysterious Nindroid power source, Zane created an icy explosion that destroyed both the enemy and himself. Zane's sacrifice was one of the bravest actions I have ever seen. He not only saved Ninjago — he saved the world.

With the Golden Master vanquished, Ninjago must once again rise from the ashes of destruction. And once again, the ninja must find their place in a new world.

Without his golden powers, Lloyd is back in his role as the Green Ninja. And without their friend Zane, the other ninja — Kai, Cole, and Jay — aren't sure what to do. They feel lost.

As much as my brother, Sensei Wu, and I wish we could step in and give the ninja direction, this is a journey they must take on their own. But we have faith that they will band together, stronger than ever. For in their hearts, they are, and always will be, ninja.

And as for Zane, well . . . he had a power source different from any other Nindroid's. His power source was a mystery. So I ask myself: How can a mystery die? I do not think it can. But I will wait and see.

Sensei Garmadon

Chapter 1

"**Ninja never quit, and ninja** will never be forgotten. Wherever you are, Zane, you'll always be one of us."

The crowd solemnly applauded as Kai finished his speech. All of the citizens of New Ninjago City were gathered to dedicate a statue in honor of Zane, the Ninja of Ice.

Zane had shown courage and selflessness unlike any other. He had used his Nindroid power source to stop the Digital Overlord from taking over the world. In a fierce battle, Zane had destroyed the Digital

Overlord with an incredible, frozen blast. But the victory came at a cost. Zane was also lost in the explosion. The citizens of New Ninjago City were very grateful to Zane for his sacrifice. They were also very sad.

Streetlights shone on the titanium statue. A light snow fell from the sky. Kai, Cole, Jay, and Lloyd stared up at it in silence for a minute. Then Kai's sister, Nya, walked up to them.

"It's a great statue," she said, placing a hand on Kai's shoulder. "Zane would have loved it."

Kai nodded. "Yeah. I think he would have."

A few days later, Cole, Jay, Kai, Lloyd, and Nya walked down the main street of New Ninjago City. Things had been ... different since the statue ceremony. They were still a team, but without Zane, things didn't feel quite the same.

"So, what should we do now?" Jay asked the others.

Kai pointed to a bright neon sign just down the road. "How about some noodles? Like old times?"

"Sounds good," agreed Cole. "I'm hungry."

"Me, too," said Jay. "Now, that's using your noodle, Kai!" Everyone groaned. Jay's bad jokes were one thing that hadn't changed.

A few minutes later, they were all seated around a table at Master Chen's Noodle House. The place was **packed**. A waiter on roller skates skidded to a stop at their table.

"Your water," he said, quickly placing a glass in front of each of them. Then he rolled away.

"Cool job," remarked Jay.

"Not as cool as being a ninja," said Cole.

Kai frowned. "Being a ninja is only cool when there's something to fight for."

Everyone grew quiet. After the first time

they had defeated the Dark Overlord, there were no bad guys for Kai, Cole, and Jay to fight anymore. So the ninja had all become teachers at Sensei Wu's Academy. But none of them were cut out to be teachers, really.

Nya pointed to the conveyor belt snaking past their table. "Come on, let's pick out our noodles!"

Steaming bowls of noodles whizzed by them. Peanut noodles, chicken noodles, tofu noodles — any kind of noodles you could think of.

"Wow, Master Chen has it all," said Cole.

"**Extra** spicy. My fave," said Kai, choosing a bowl topped with red chili peppers. As the Ninja of Fire, he liked things hot — even his food.

Jay grabbed a bowl of chicken noodles and placed it in front of Nya.

"And here's *your* favorite," he said.

"Actually, Jay, I was going to get the veggie noodles," Nya said.

"*I* know she likes veggie noodles," Cole muttered.

Jay spun around. "What did you say, Cole?"

Nya got a nervous look on her face. Not long ago, she and Jay had been boyfriend and girlfriend — sort of. Nya had been too busy being Samurai X, and Jay was too busy being the Ninja of Lightning for them to go out on dates or anything. But they liked each other.

Then Nya had taken a silly computer test at the headquarters of Borg Industries. The computer calculated her perfect match — and it was Cole!

That had left Nya **confused**. Jay and Cole had found out about the test, and now they were confused, too. They had asked Nya to choose between them, and she couldn't.

"I'll have the chicken noodles, too," Nya said quickly, taking the bowl from Jay.

"Tofu for me!" Lloyd exclaimed. "Let's eat!"

Everybody began to loudly slurp their noodles. There were so many bowls on the table, it was difficult to tell whose was whose. Cole reached over to one with his chopsticks.

"Hey, those are my noodles!" Jay cried.

"Whoa, sorry." Cole jerked back. "Relax, it's just noodles."

Jay's cheeks turned hot. "Sure, take my noodles, just like you took my girlfriend."

"I didn't take anything! Nya hasn't decided yet!" Cole reminded him.

Nya quickly changed the subject. "So, now that there aren't any bad guys anymore, I guess we'll all go back to teaching at Sensei Wu's Academy, right? Those kids are pretty cute, after all."

That took the ninja by surprise.

Kai swallowed slowly and shook his head. "I don't know, sis. I mean, things are different now."

Cole nodded. "Yeah, the *staff* isn't like it used to be." He pointed at Jay. "I'm not going back unless you choose between me and him."

That made Jay super-angry. "Why should Nya have to choose? She never actually broke up with me. So technically, she hasn't *un*chosen me!"

Jay slammed his hand down on the table. His noodle bowl **flew up** in the air.

Plop! It landed on Cole's head.

"Oh, so that's how you want to do it, is it?" Cole asked. He dumped a bowl of noodles right onto Jay's lap.

"Hey, I just washed these pants!" Jay cried. He jumped up on his chair and grabbed two noodle bowls off the conveyor belt. *"Aaaaiya!"*

He sent the bowls flying at Cole, who ducked. They hit a roller-skating server, sending him speeding into *another* roller-skating server. The tray she was carrying fell out of her hands, spilling water everywhere!

"Whoa!" Another waiter slipped in the water and went flying! Lloyd leaped up and caught him before he fell.

Suddenly, two burly guys in black suits appeared at the table.

"I'm afraid we're going to have to ask you to —"

"Leave," Kai finished for him. "We got it. Come on, guys."

Cole looked longingly at the messy pile of noodles on the table. "But I haven't finished yet."

Outside, Nya tried to smooth things over. "Let's go to the academy and talk about this," she said. "I'm sure we can work it out. We always do."

"No way," said Jay, angry and hurt. "I've had enough. Zane's gone and our 'team' isn't a team anymore. Things can't magically go back to the way they were. I'm outta here."

"At least that's one thing we agree on," Cole said heatedly. They both **stormed off** in different directions.

Nya sighed and turned to Kai and Lloyd. "Well, I guess that just leaves us."

To Nya's surprise, Kai shook his head. "Sorry, sis. I can't go back there right now, either. Too many memories. Maybe Jay is right. Maybe what we all need now is a fresh start."

He walked off without another word.

Nya and Lloyd looked at each other.

Were the ninja really splitting up?

Chapter 2

The next morning, Lloyd walked through the city's downtown. Residents had already started to rebuild after the big battle with the Golden Master. Some people were doing it the old-fashioned way: with bricks and cement. Other workers were laying lines of digital cable.

Looks like a blend of the old and the new, Lloyd thought.

Old and new. Before and after. Before the Digital Overlord, Lloyd was the Golden Ninja. He was a hero in New Ninjago City, riding through the skies on his Golden Dragon.

During the battle, Lloyd had to give up his Golden Powers. Now he was the Green Ninja again. Not that there was anything wrong with being the Green Ninja. He loved being on a team with Kai, Cole, Jay, and Zane.

But was there even a **team anymore**?

Lloyd stopped in front of Borg Industries' headquarters. "I wonder what Cyrus is up to."

Cyrus Borg was a genius, the mastermind behind New Ninjago City. Under his hand, the city had become fully computerized.

And that was pretty great — until the Overlord infected the system with a computer virus. The Digital Overlord had taken Borg over, transforming him into a half-man, half-droid.

But now he was the old Cyrus again. Lloyd pushed open the glass doors of the building.

The lobby inside was eerily quiet.

"Hello?" Lloyd called out.

His voice bounced off the walls. Curious, Lloyd rode up the elevator to Cyrus Borg's floor.

The elevator stopped and the doors slid open.

"Help! Help!"

Lloyd knew that voice. It was Cyrus! With ninja speed, he raced toward the cries and through a door marked "Testing Room."

Floating in the center of the room was a giant Nindroid! Its black, armored body shimmered with a strange glow. Streaks of red light poured from its one red eye. Lightning sparked in the air all around it.

Cyrus Borg was frantically steering his wheelchair around the room, trying to avoid the lightning blasts.

"Lloyd! Quickly! The red lever!" he yelled.

Lloyd spotted the lever on the wall across the room. "Got it!"

He sprang up and somersaulted through the air as lightning whizzed past him.

Bam! He kicked the lever on his way down. Instantly, the lightning stopped — and the Nindroid vanished.

"Oh, thank you, Lloyd," Cyrus said, out of breath as he wheeled up to him.

"What was that?" Lloyd asked.

"It's a holographic training system I'm developing," the inventor replied. "As you can see, it has a few glitches. It's a good thing you came when you did."

"So that Nindroid wasn't real?" Lloyd asked.

Cyrus shook his head. "No. But it will be an ideal training tool, don't you think?" He looked to where the hologram had vanished. "At least, it will be once it's perfected. So, Lloyd, what brings you here?"

Lloyd wasn't exactly sure himself. "I guess I just wanted to see if anything new was happening."

Cyrus adjusted his glasses. "Well, this is new." He gestured to the hologram device. "But it's not quite ready yet. When it is, I'd like to bring in you and the ninja team to test it out for me. What do you say?"

"Yeah, right, the team." Lloyd shuffled awkwardly.

Cyrus didn't seem to notice Lloyd's hesitation. "Excellent! I shall call on you soon," he said. "Thank you again for your help."

Lloyd left Cyrus and went back out into the streets of New Ninjago City. If Cyrus wanted the team, Lloyd would bring him the team. He only had one problem.

He had no idea where they were!

Chapter 3

The sun blazed down on Jay as he walked across the Sea of Sand. The colorful neon sign for Ed and Edna's "Scrap N Junk" glowed in the distance. Jay hadn't seen his mom and dad in a while. They would probably have some good advice for him. They always did.

As he got closer, Jay saw that the junkyard was hopping. Usually, he'd find his mom or dad tinkering with one of the busted vehicles. The only visitors were crows that came

to perch on top of tall metal towers made out of scrap.

But now the place was filled with people. It looked like they were building stuff — robots — using pieces of scrap from around the yard.

Jay walked through the archway and stopped a woman carrying a small motor and a metal garbage can lid.

"What's going on?" he asked.

"It's the **Junkbot Battle Supreme**!" she replied. "Are you competing?"

Jay shook his head. "No, I was just looking for my —"

"Jay! My little bird has come back to the nest!" a voice called out.

Jay turned to see his mom, Edna, hurrying toward him with her arms open. She squeezed him in a big hug.

"Ed! Jay's here!" she yelled.

A white-haired man walked up, wiping his hands on an oily rag.

"Well, hello there, son," he said. "I am so sorry to hear about Zane."

"He was a lovely boy, and a hero," added Edna.

Jay nodded. "Thanks, he was."

"So, what's new in the ninja business?" Ed asked.

"Nothing much," Jay replied. "But what's all this about a Junkbot Battle?"

Edna smiled brightly. "Isn't it a fantastic idea? Competitors have forty-eight hours to build a robot using the junk in the yard."

"Then tomorrow they'll face off in a series of battles until there's one ultimate winner," said Ed. "Should be a **rootin' tootin'** fun time!"

Jay suddenly felt excited. "Hey, can I build one?" he asked. He had grown up in the junkyard, inventing things. It always made him happy.

"Well, you won't have much time, son," Ed replied. "The battles start tomorrow morning."

"No problem!" Jay said. "I'll work fast."

Edna pinched his cheek. "That's my son. Such an eager little beaver!"

Jay blushed. His mom always embarrassed him in front of his friends.

Then he remembered — none of his friends were around to see this.

"I'd better get to work," Jay said. He gazed at the towers of junk piled up everywhere. There were junked cars, shiny hubcaps, broken tools, wires, tubes — everything he would need.

He grinned. **"This is going to be awesome!"**

"Welcome to the first annual Junkbot Battle Supreme!" Ed announced into a microphone the next morning. "Our first challenger is ten-

year-old Suzie Wheeler, and her Junkbot, Mr. Peepers!"

The crowd **cheered** as a young girl stepped into the battle arena with her tiny Junkbot. Mr. Peepers had the body of a toaster set on top of four wheels. Two metal stalks stuck out of one end of the toaster. Each one was tipped with a round ball painted to look like an eye.

"And facing her is Jay Walker and his Junkbot, Ninjasaur!"

Jay stepped out into the arena, waving and bowing. He was really proud of his Junkbot.

Ninjasaur stomped out behind Jay. Twice as tall as him, it looked like a metal T. rex with a blue stripe painted down its back. Jay had added all kinds of sweet tricks to it. Ninjasaur could breathe fire and was programmed to perform the coolest ninja moves.

He took a look at Mr. Peepers and felt sorry for little Suzie.

"Don't worry, I won't be too hard on you!" he called out.

"I'm not worried!" Suzie called back. "Maybe *you're* the one who should be worried."

Jay laughed. *What a cute kid,* he thought. *I'll try not to completely wreck Mr. Peepers. I just need to knock it out so I can head to the next round.*

"Let the Junkbot Battle begin!" Ed yelled.

Suzie's eyes narrowed. She turned the knob on her remote control and Mr. Peepers wheeled across the battle arena.

"Ninjasaur, crush!" Jay commanded, pressing some buttons on his controls. Ninjasaur stomped forward. Jay just had to bring one heavy foot down on Mr. Peepers, and it would be over.

Stomp! Jay waited to hear the crushing sound, but it didn't come.

Stomp! Ninjasaur stomped again, but he still didn't get Mr. Peepers. The tiny bot raced circles around him.

"Ninjasaur, stop!" Jay called out. He had to rethink his strategy. Maybe he could aim a fire blast at Mr. Peepers . . .

But where *was* the tiny Junkbot?

Suddenly, Ninjasaur started to spark and sizzle. Across the arena, Suzie had broken out into a wicked grin.

"What's happening?" Jay asked. And then he saw it — Mr. Peepers was right under Ninjasaur's tail, shooting electric blasts out of its toast slots.

"Ninjasaur, flip!" Jay cried, punching in new commands.

The metal dino crouched down, and then sprang into an amazing backflip.

Boom! The ground shook when it landed. Mr. Peepers quickly zipped out from underneath it. But Suzie didn't look worried.

Jay punched another button. "Ninjasaur, flame!"

Ninjsaur's mouth opened wide . . . and a stream of oil poured out.

"Wait, what?" Jay asked. He frantically started pressing buttons. Ninjasaur stomped around, waving his tiny arms. Then the bot stepped right into the oil slick.

Boom! Ninjasaur crashed down hard on its back. Mr. Peepers wheeled right up onto his face.

Zap! Zap! Zap! Jay watched helplessly as the little toaster bot blasted Ninjasaur. The big bot started to sizzle and shake. Then it stopped moving. Black smoke poured from its nostrils.

"Mr. Peepers wins!" Ed yelled, and the crowd cheered. Suzie walked up to Jay and held out her hand.

"Nice try," she said.

Jay shook her hand. "Yeah, thanks."

He patted Ninjasaur's smoking head. "It's back to the scrap heap for you, buddy!"

Chapter 4

Sparks were flying outside New Ninjago City, too, at the Heart of Steel Foundry. Inside, giant kettles bubbled with superhot liquid metal. Workers in head-to-toe fireproof suits melted scrap and poured it into molds to make machine parts.

"We're rebuilding Ninjago piece by piece," the foreman told Kai when he had applied for the job. "But those kettles can reach almost three thousand degrees. I hope you can take the heat."

Kai grinned. "No problem!"

Now Kai stirred a steaming, sparking kettle of molten metal. He wore a silver fireproof suit and a protective shield over his face. As he stared into the bubbling, orange goo, it almost hypnotized him.

For the first time in days, he felt relaxed. *I'm not going to do this forever,* he thought. *I just need a break. A break from Jay and Cole fighting. A break from missing Zane . . .*

Suddenly, someone bumped into him from behind. Kai almost toppled into the kettle, but he stopped himself just in time.

"Hey, watch where you're going, buddy!" Kai cried.

The worker who had bumped into him turned. He had a thick head of hair and reminded Kai of a big, angry bear.

"Who you calling buddy, *buddy*?" the burly man **growled**.

"Listen, dude, I almost fell into that vat," Kai said, pointing.

The big guy laughed. "What's the matter, you can't take the **heat**?"

Kai's eyes flashed angrily. "Oh, I can take the heat. Nobody takes the heat like I can!"

The man leaned right in Kai's face. "Break room. Noon," he hissed.

Kai wondered what the guy had in mind. Was he looking for trouble? *Well, his mistake,* Kai thought. The guy didn't realize there was a ninja under Kai's big silver suit. But, boy, would he find out!

When the lunch whistle rang, Kai headed for the break room.

The big guy was sitting at a table, surrounded by some of the other foundry workers. He had two bottles of hot sauce in front of him.

Kai took the seat across from him, and the big guy slid one of the bottles over.

"First one to stop loses," he challenged.

Kai grinned and picked up the bottle. "It won't be me!" he bragged.

Kai looked at the label: "Captain Vick's Impossibly Hot Volcano Juice."

Ha! Silly name, Kai thought. *This is going to be easy.*

A short guy walked up to referee the competition. "Ready, set . . . go!"

Kai picked up the bottle and started to chug. At first, he didn't feel anything. But a few seconds later . . . *bam!* A searing heat filled his mouth and poured down his throat. It was like he was drinking fire!

He paused for a split second and took a look at his opponent. The big guy's face was bright red. But he wasn't giving up.

Fighting back tears, Kai kept chugging. So what if it was hot? He was the **Ninja of Fire**! He could take it!

But the heat got worse and worse. Sweat poured out of him like water from a fire hose. He was about to give up, when . . .

Slam! The big guy pounded the bottle on the table. It still had an inch of hot sauce

left in it. He looked like he was going to explode.

"He's done!" somebody yelled.

Kai finished his bottle and slammed it down. "I win!" he yelled.

Whoosh! A flame came right out of his mouth! It flew across the table and took off the top of the big guy's wavy hair. It left him with a big, bald stripe!

The guy stood up. "That. Was. Not. Cool."

Then he lunged across the table.

Kai jumped up, ready to deliver a drop-kick. But suddenly, he stopped.

He was a ninja. He should be fighting evil guys trying to take over the world, not getting into scraps with regular guys over who could drink the most hot sauce.

Zane wouldn't want this.

Kai landed and swiftly left the room. Working at the steel factory had been fun, but it wasn't worth getting into trouble over.

There must be something better out there.

Chapter 5

ar away, Cole trekked across a wide meadow. He couldn't stop thinking about what had happened in the noodle shop. Even though he was angry, the fight had been silly. What kind of ninja got into a noodle fight?

Not the old Cole. The old Cole was sturdy and strong and calm.

But new Cole — new Cole's head wasn't right since this Nya thing. If he was being completely honest with himself, he wasn't even sure if he liked her that way. But why shouldn't he? Nya was awesome. She was smart and nice and funny, and she had amazing samurai skills. So when it seemed like maybe she liked him, well, it was hard to explain how that made him feel.

I just need to get away from it all, Cole thought as he hiked toward a **thick forest**. He wore a red plaid shirt and carried a dark backpack. It held all the supplies he would need for a few days.

Butterflies passed as he traipsed through the tall grass. Then he came to the edge of a dense, green pine grove.

It was different here. He could feel it. Pine needles crunched under his feet, and a peaceful quiet filled the air. Cole was the Ninja of Earth, and this place felt just right to him.

"Time for lunch," Cole said. He opened his backpack and rummaged through it, pulling out a broccoli and peanut butter sandwich he had made earlier that morning. He had never eaten one before, but he liked

broccoli and he liked peanut butter, so why not?

"And there's nobody here to make fun of my cooking," he muttered as he carefully spread out a cloth napkin on a flat rock. Whenever he cooked for the ninja, they always complained about his food. Well, those days were over!

"There's nothing like being out in nature!" Cole said loudly, gazing up at the trees.

He placed the sandwich on the napkin and then went to the stream to get some clean water. But when he came back, the sandwich was gone!

"What the —?" Cole asked. And then he saw it. A squirrel sat on a tree stump, clutching the sandwich in its paws.

"Hey, that's my lunch!" Cole cried.

He lunged for the squirrel, but the critter jumped off the stump. It put the sandwich between its teeth and scurried up a tree.

Cole scrambled after it. The squirrel stopped on a branch, took the sandwich out of its mouth, and made a noise that sounded a lot like laughter.

Is this squirrel mocking me? Cole wondered.

"Gotcha!" Cole yelled, reaching for the sandwich. But three woodpeckers flew out of nowhere and started pecking at him.

"Hey, quit it!" Cole cried. "Stop it right — *whoa!*"

Cole tumbled out of the tree. Luckily, he wasn't too high up. He landed with a soft thud on a bed of pine needles.

He jumped to his feet. "Very funny! I'll — *whoa!*"

Cole tripped and fell flat on his face. Looking back, he saw two chipmunks holding a stick by his feet. They had tripped him on purpose!

"That wasn't very nice," Cole scolded as

they scampered off. He got back on his feet and looked up. The squirrel sat on the branch, still holding the sandwich.

"Just give it back!" he pleaded.

Thud! A blue jay flew past, slamming into him. He fell backward again.

"Ow!" This time, he landed on something sharp. He craned his neck.

He had landed right on top of a **porcupine**!

"Ow! Ow! Ow!" Cole cried, pulling the sharp spines out of his pants. The squirrel stayed on the branch, chattering.

"Fine!" Cole called. "Eat it! It's yours!"

The squirrel held the sandwich up to its mouth and began to nibble. Then it stopped.

"Squeak!" It made a face and threw the sandwich off the branch. Cole's sandwich was disgusting even to a squirrel.

"Not you, too," Cole said with a sigh.

Maybe getting back to nature wasn't going to work out after all.

Chapter 6

Jay slumped across the couch in his parents' trailer. The TV set blared on the other side of the room.

Ed and Edna walked in.

"There's my boy," said Jay's mom. "But what's with that frown?"

"Do you have to ask?" Jay moaned. "My awesome Ninjasaur was beaten by a tiny Junkbot named Mr. Peepers. It was humiliating!"

"Oh, it wasn't so bad," Edna said.

"Actually, that was pretty embarrassing, son," Ed pointed out. "Did you see that little guy? He zapped your dino pretty darned good."

"Yes, I know!" Jay said, pulling a pillow over his face.

"Well, you didn't have as much time as the others to work on your Junkbot," Edna reminded him. "And you're a good inventor, but that's not what you're best at. You're best at being a ninja. The Ninja of Lightning."

Jay peeked out from the pillow. "What good is being a ninja without a bad guy to fight?" *Or a team . . . or Zane,* he thought miserably.

"Jay, you don't need a bad guy to fight if you want to do good in the world," his mom said. "You will always be a ninja, no matter what you do."

Ed settled into an armchair. "Speaking of ninja, my favorite show is coming on!" He turned up the volume on the TV.

"Who out there is Ninjago's next hero?" an announcer's voice blared from the television. "Who has it in them to be . . ."

"*Ninjaaa . . . Now!*" yelled the audience.

Jay sat up. "What is this?"

"Only the best game show ever," Edna said, sitting on the couch next to him. "Haven't you seen it? The contestants face the Gauntlet of Humility."

"It's an obstacle course, and, boy, is it a doozy!" Ed added. "Nobody ever makes it all the way to the end!"

A man in a black tux came on the screen. "I'm Fred Finley, your host. Let's see who will be Ninjago's next hero — and whose dreams will be gone in a **flash**!"

Jay watched, fascinated, as the first contestant approached the Gauntlet. She ran across a wall while guys dressed as monkeys threw giant stuffed bananas at her. She kept her balance and sprinted wildly to a spinning platform. Then she ran through a

tunnel, dodging a huge foam boulder that rolled through it. Finally, she zip-lined over a pool filled with chocolate pudding ... but she lost her grip and tumbled in! *Splat!*

Jay's eyes were wide with excitement. "Hey, I could do that!" he said.

"Of course you could, son," Edna said.

"I bet you'd be the first one to make it to the end of the course," Ed added.

Jay nodded. "Yeah, I bet I would."

Maybe he didn't need a team to be a ninja. Maybe he could be the most awesome ninja ever ... !

One week later, Jay was on the set of *Ninjaaa ... Now!* He wore elbow- and knee-pads over a blue padded suit, and a white helmet. In front of him loomed the giant Gauntlet of Humility. Soon, he would be conquering it!

The show's producer, Rachel Sparrow, walked up to Jay.

"We're very excited to have you on the show," she said. "A real ninja! You're a perfect match for the game."

"Yeah, a perfect match," Jay repeated, suddenly thinking of Nya. He used to think maybe he was *her* perfect match, but now . . . He pushed away the thought. He had a game show to win!

"So, because you're a *real* ninja, we've pumped up the Gauntlet for you a bit," Rachel said.

"Pumped it up?" Jay asked.

"You're going to love it," Rachel assured him. "Now, go get 'em!"

Fred Finley was standing in front of the Gauntlet.

"Who will be Ninjago's next hero, and whose dreams will be gone in a flash?" he asked, and the crowd cheered. "Let's meet our first contestant. You know him as the

Ninja of Lightning. Does he have what it takes to be *Ninjaaa . . . Now!*? Please welcome Jay Walker!"

Jay jogged out to the Gauntlet, pumping his fists in the air.

"Hey, Fred," he said. "How's it going?"

"Great!" Fred replied. "I get to say the same thing over and over every day, and I can't stop smiling! See this smile? I've had it for seventeen days. Can't get rid of it."

"Uh, yeah," Jay said. "So, I'm ready for the Gauntlet!"

"And the Gauntlet is ready for you," Fred told him. "Just for you, we've pumped up our Gauntlet with super extra mega power!"

"Oooooooooooooh," said the crowd.

"Super extra mega power"? Jay didn't like the sound of that. But he didn't let on.

"Yeah, like I'm worried about a bunch of monkeys," Jay said. He turned to the crowd. "Do you know why monkeys like bananas? Because they have *appeal*!"

44

Everybody laughed. That was all Jay needed to hear. He took the microphone.

"Speaking of bananas, what did one banana say to the other banana? *Yel-low!* Get it?" The crowd laughed again. From the sidelines, Rachel gave him a thumbs-up.

Fred took the mic back from him. "Very funny, Jay. Now it's time to get started. Climb up to the first platform!"

As Jay began to walk to the stairs, he had an idea. The show wanted a real ninja? He'd show them a **real ninja**! He turned and faced the audience.

"I don't need the stairs," he said, and he held out his arms, palms facing down. "This is how the Ninja of Lightning does it!"

Zzzzzzzzzap! Arcs of lightning shot straight down from his palms, propelling him up. The crowd went wild, cheering him the whole way. Jay stepped onto the platform.

"Okay!" Fred said below. "Start the Doomsday Clock!"

A clock with colorful flashing lights descended from the ceiling. The big, yellow neon hand started to tick. Jay waved at the crowd one last time before he headed out onto the Monkey Wall.

"Ready, set . . . *Ninjaaaaaaaaaaaa . . . NOW!*" cried Fred.

Jay began **racing across the wall**. He could see the guys dressed as monkeys down below. He kept his balance, but the guys weren't even throwing bananas yet.

"What are you waiting for? Quit monkeying around!" Jay yelled down.

Then he saw several yellow objects flying up at him. Yellow . . . and orange . . . and red? As the first one whizzed past his face, he felt a wave of heat.

"Holy flaming bananas!" Jay yelled.

Now he *really* didn't like the sound of *super extra mega power*!

Chapter 7

 ai found Nya at Sensei Wu's Academy.

"What's up, big brother?" she asked him hopefully. "Are you back? For good?"

"No, I just wanted to see you," Kai said. "I can't stay here. It's just not the same with-out . . . the other guys."

"Maybe if you come back, they will, too," Nya urged.

"Why should I be the first one to come back?" Kai asked stubbornly. "Jay and Cole are the ones who started this whole thing.

Actually, *you* started it when you took that dumb test."

Nya held up her hands. "Hey, back off," she said. "I'm not some emotionless droid. I have **complicated feelings**. That's just how it is."

Kai sighed. "Yeah, I guess," he said. "Anyway, I got this job at the steel foundry, which was awesome, because it was super-hot in there and I got to work with metal again, like when we were little. But then I got into a fight with this hotheaded guy, and —"

"Kai, maybe you need to cool down," Nya told him. "You know, chill out for a while. Meditate and try to figure things out. That's what Zane would tell you to do."

Kai nodded. "Yeah, you're right," he said. "I guess I just don't know where to start."

He sighed, and his eyes wandered to a flyer on the academy bulletin board.

"NINJAGO ICE RINK. FIRST SKATING LESSON FREE!"

"Ice rink," he said thoughtfully. "That's a cool place."

"Well, I didn't mean *literally* cool —" Nya began, but Kai was already heading out.

"Thanks, Nya!" he called behind him.

"Clear the ice, please! Clear the ice, please!" a mechanical voice blared over the speakers in the Ninjago Ice Rink.

Kai loved his new job! He got to ride the Rambooni, the big machine that smoothed out the ice after people had been skating on it for a long time. The hum of the engine was soothing. It felt good to see the ice get nice and smooth after the machine passed over it. He definitely felt a lot calmer.

"Nya would be proud," he said out loud as he mounted the Rambooni. *And Zane would be, too,* he thought. He never went very long without thinking about his lost friend.

Kai settled into the seat and started the engine. The rink workers cleared the ice. Skaters eagerly waited outside the barriers for the ice to be ready again.

"Won't be long!" Kai called out cheerfully. Then he steered out onto the rink, slowly making his way across and back again.

He actually found himself humming as he worked.

I could get used to this, he thought.

As he made another turn, he spotted something across the rink. A dad and a bunch of kids were skating on the ice, over by the party area. It was the dad's son's birthday. They were supposed to wait like everyone else for the ice to be smoothed out. A rink worker yelled at them to get off the ice. But the dad just ignored him.

Kai felt a flare of anger. "Hey!" he yelled. "You're putting those kids in danger!"

The dad didn't even look at him. All Kai could see was the back of his bald head.

Kai forgot about his smooth back-and-forth motion. He zigzagged across the ice toward the dad. One of the workers was getting the kids out of the way. But the dad wouldn't budge.

Kai stopped the engine. "Hey! You need to get off the ice!" he yelled.

The dad turned around. Kai recognized his big, angry face. It was the guy from the steel foundry!

"You!" the guy growled.

"You!" Kai cried. "What are you doing? Just get off the ice!"

"Are you going to make me?" the guy asked.

Kai jumped off the Rambooni. Every ounce of peace and calm had left his body. **"Are you serious?** This is a family place! Back off, dude!"

The guy was about to charge when Kai heard a groan behind him. He had forgotten to put the brakes on the Rambooni! The giant machine slid forward.

"No!" Kai cried. He tried to jump up into the driver's seat, but he slipped and fell on the ice.

Crash! The Rambooni smashed right into the party area, **crushing** a pile of presents and knocking the birthday cake off the table. The dad's face was purple with anger. He stomped up to Kai and lifted him up with two fingers.

"Meet me at the Yang Tavern at midnight," he said. "We're going to settle this once and for all!"

Chapter

8

ole picked up the broccoli and peanut butter sandwich that the squirrel had tossed.

"Five second rule," he muttered, and took a bite out of it. "I don't see why that squirrel didn't like it. It's not bad."

He finished the sandwich and packed up his backpack.

Might as well head back to the city, he thought, when he suddenly heard the hum of machinery from somewhere in the woods.

Curious, he followed the sound. The soft pine trees at the edge of the forest gave way

to towering trees with trunks as thick as houses. The bark was deep, ebony black.

"Blackwood Forest," Cole said out loud. "I've heard of this place."

He kept walking, and the sound got louder. Soon he saw the source: a huge lumberjack camp. Lumberjacks high up in the trees hacked away at thick branches with axes. Others on the ground loaded the branches onto powerful trucks with humming motors.

Cole stared at them for a few minutes, just watching. They worked like a well-oiled team. The axmen hacked at the trunks. Others attached the trees onto long pike poles and dragged them to the trucks. The next group loaded them.

The way the lumberjacks all worked together, trusting one another, reminded Cole of Kai, Jay, Zane, and Lloyd. They used to be a team. A great team. He missed them. But was he ready to be on a team again?

"Lookin' for work?"

Cole jumped at the voice next to him. A guy in a flannel shirt and hard hat was talking to him.

"I'm the foreman here. We could use another hand," he said.

Cole was surprised. But it sounded like a good idea. "Uh, sure," he said.

The foreman held out his hand. "Nice to have you as part of the crew."

The foreman handed him an axe, and Cole joined a group of lumberjacks chopping through one of the thick tree trunks. With his superstrength, he could have hacked through the trunk in about three strokes. But he didn't want to stand out. So he kept the pace with everyone else.

The other lumberjacks didn't talk much. They mostly grunted. A few hours into the job, one of the guys nodded to the foreman.

"When's dinner?" he asked.

"Not sure," the foreman replied. "Old

Cookie got a splinter this morning. He's down for the count."

"I can cook dinner," Cole offered.

"Sure," the foreman said, and that was it.

A short while later, Cole made his way to the cook's trailer. He couldn't find "Old Cookie," but he did find shelves loaded with canned fruits and vegetables. He stared at it all for a moment.

"Lumberjack Stew," he said out loud. "That'll be perfect! I can use some canned hot dogs, and some ketchup, and maybe some brussels sprouts and horseradish . . ."

An hour later, Cole had a big pot of his Lumberjack Stew bubbling over an open **campfire** . He felt pretty proud. It smelled a little weird, but he was sure it was going to be delicious.

"Come and get it!" he yelled, ringing the dinner bell.

The lumberjacks came in from the deep woods, and Cole spooned out bowls of

steaming stew for every-
one. He watched nervously as they dug in.
Would they hate it, like his friends always did?

Nobody said anything. All he could hear
were loud slurping sounds.

He walked up to one of the guys. "So, how
do you like it?" Cole asked.

The lumberjack shrugged. "It's fine."

Cole should have felt good. Instead, he
felt strangely empty. Jay would have said
something like, "Cole, this is more like
Lumberjack Goo!" Or Kai would say, "Even
the Great Devourer wouldn't eat this junk!"
Lloyd would laugh so hard that stew would
come out of his nose. And Zane, being Zane,
wouldn't have really understood the joke.

"Ah, well, I guess it's good that it came
out ... good," Cole said with a sigh. He started
washing the dirty dishes in a big tub of water.

After dinner, the camp was eerily quiet.
The guys were sitting around campfires,
but nobody was talking or singing or telling

jokes. A few of them were whittling sticks of wood.

Cole sat next to one of them. "So, what are you making?" he asked.

"A skinnier stick," the guy replied, not even looking up.

Cole raised his voice. "Anybody know any good **jokes**?" he asked, but all he got in reply were a few coughs.

Cole sighed. Maybe it was better this way. No attachments. No friendships. Just do your job and that was that. Easier not to get hurt.

Suddenly, Cole heard a chattering sound behind him. It was the squirrel from earlier!

"Shouldn't you be asleep?" Cole asked.

The squirrel hopped onto the now-cooled stewpot. It scooped up some stew with its paw and tasted it.

The squirrel made a face. It stuck its tongue out, put a paw over its heart, and fell off the edge of the pot.

"Oh, no!" cried Cole. His stew had killed the squirrel! He went to help it. But the little squirrel jumped up, chattered some more, and scampered off.

"Very funny," Cole said flatly. Although he had to admit that it had cheered him up.

Deep down, just a little, he missed the joking around.

Deep down, he missed his friends.

Chapter 9

Jay ducked as another flaming banana whizzed past him. His mind raced as he tried to figure out what to do.

If only Zane were here, he thought. *He would freeze them. Or Kai could absorb them. Heck, Cole would probably eat them. But I can't do any of those things!*

But he could run fast — and duck. Jay made his way across the top of the narrow wall as quickly as he could, ducking and dodging the fiery, fruity missiles.

"Look at Jay go!" Fred Finley cried, and the audience cheered.

Jay reached the end of the wall and gazed down at the spinning platform below. He looked left and right. No more flaming bananas. Maybe this part would be easy. He jumped down onto the platform . . .

. . . and his feet slipped from underneath him! They had greased the surface! Still on his belly, Jay slid across the slick platform, seconds away from **falling off**.

Cole's superstrength would come in handy now, he thought. *He could stop this platform from spinning with one tight grip.*

But Cole wasn't around. Jay had to do this on his own. Right before he fell, he gripped the edge of the platform with both hands. He hung on as tightly as he could as his legs flew out straight behind him.

The crowd cheered him on. There was no use climbing back onto the platform.

He had to think of his next goal — the tunnel.

He had to time it just right. The platform spun in fast circles, passing the tunnel entrance every few seconds. He'd have to make one perfect leap . . . but luckily, that was something he was good at.

Jay counted in his head. *One . . . two . . .* and then he let go, somersaulting in the air and landing at the tunnel entrance.

"Look at Jay fly!" Fred Finley crowed. "He's conquered our extreme slippery platform!"

"Jay! Jay! Jay!" the crowd chanted.

Jay's heart was pounding. This was **pretty fun**! Now he had to run through the tunnel and avoid the big boulder that rolled through it. That should be pretty easy if he stuck to the sides.

He ran in, and saw the boulder speeding toward him. He flattened himself against the wall of the tunnel. The foam rock easily rolled past him. Piece of cake!

Then he heard a rumbling. Another, bigger boulder rolled toward him! There was no room to get past!

"That's not extreme — that's just not fair!" Jay cried.

He weighed his options. He could run back out of the tunnel entrance, but that would make him look cowardly. If only there was another way . . .

Zap! Jay quickly hit the ceiling of the tunnel with a lightning blast, opening a hole for him to climb through. He jumped up and landed on top of the tunnel.

"He's escaped the **Boulder of Doom**! Amazing!" Fred Finley cried.

"Jay! Jay! Jay!" the crowd cheered.

Jay sprinted across the top of the tunnel and jumped down to grab the handle of the zip line. He just had to shoot across the giant vat of chocolate pudding.

"Jay! Jay! Jay!"

"Time for this bird to fly!" Jay called out,

and he launched across the pudding vat. Suddenly . . .

Bonk! A huge stuffed ball swung through the air, hitting him! It caught him off guard.

"Whoa!" Jay yelled.

Sploooshh! Jay and the giant ball landed in the vat of chocolate pudding. A huge wave of pudding splattered everywhere, engulfing the announcer, Fred Finley!

Jay popped up at the surface of the chocolate pudding pool. His heart sank. He had failed the Gauntlet. After all that, it was over. But still, he thought, he had to make the best of it. Jay climbed out of the pool and licked his arm.

"Tasty!" he said, and everybody laughed.

Fred Finley, however, was *not* happy. He stomped past him, covered in chocolate pudding. His seventeen-day smile had finally faded.

"That's it!" he yelled. "This job is the worst! I quit!"

He tossed down his microphone and stormed off.

"Cut!" a voice yelled, and Rachel Sparrow came running out.

"Sorry about that," said Jay.

"Don't worry," said Rachel. "Fred's always throwing tantrums. But in fact, I have a great idea. The crowd loves you. How would you like to be the new host of *Ninjaaa . . . Now!*?"

"Who, me?" Jay asked.

"Sure!" she replied. "You could crack jokes, talk to contestants . . . you'll be great."

Jay could see it in his mind. He'd be a TV star! Telling jokes that everybody laughed at. Putting on a great show. Pretty cool.

Not as cool as being a ninja, a voice inside him said. *Not as cool as being on a team.*

But Jay pushed the voice aside.

"I'll do it!"

Kai made his way down the dark alley. It hadn't been easy finding the address of the Yang Tavern. He'd had to ask around.

He wasn't sure why he had decided to meet the big, burly guy, but he figured he'd better go. The dude seemed to be popping up in his life. If they didn't settle things now, who knew what could happen the next time they met? Maybe they could talk it out over some peanuts and root beer.

Kai pushed open the door, and every eye in the place turned to look at him. A lot of the

eyes were yellow or green, because the Yang Tavern was packed with **Serpentine**. There were blue Hypnobrai, red Fangpyres, green Venomari, and black Constrictai with spikes running down their spines.

Others had bulging, red eyes — these were skeleton warriors from the Underworld. And some were regular old human eyes, attached to guys with big muscles and lots of scars. This place was a hangout for bad guys!

Some of the dudes sat at tables, drinking root beer, while others were gathered around a circular pit.

A **Slither Pit**, Kai realized. The Serpentine used these to settle disputes or decide who would be their next leader. Suddenly, he had an idea why the big guy had wanted to meet him here.

"You!"

The booming voice came from inside the pit. Kai peered over the edge. It was the big guy.

"Let's settle this once and for all," the guy said.

The pit-watchers started to hiss and cheer.

"Listen, dude, I don't think you understand," Kai said. "I'm a ninja. I've got special powers and stuff. I can't fight you. It wouldn't be fair."

"I'm not afraid of no ninja," the guy said.

Kai sighed. He didn't want to fight an ordinary dad. His ninja powers were meant for battling **evil guys** and Nindroids. He was about to turn and walk out when he felt a shove on his back.

"Whoa!" Kai toppled into the pit.

He scrambled to his feet as the guy lunged at him. The crowd started chanting the guy's name.

"Big Dan! Big Dan! Big Dan!"

"Can't we work this out over a mug of root beer?" Kai asked, dodging him.

Big Dan moved to punch Kai, and Kai dodged again. This was going to be harder than he thought. But he wasn't about to use Spinjitzu on a normal person.

Then he heard Sensei Wu's voice in his head.

Use your enemy's strength against him.

"That could work," Kai muttered.

He faced Big Dan. **"Come and get me!"** Kai taunted.

Big Dan charged across the Slither Pit like an angry bull. Just as he neared, Kai dodged to the side.

Bam! Big Dan hit the side of the Slither Pit, hard. He went down. Kai jumped up on top of him and pulled Big Dan's arms behind his back.

"What do you say we have that root beer now?" Kai asked.

Big Dan groaned, and two Constrictai came into the pit and dragged him away to the area where knocked-out contestants recovered. Kai was about to jump out when he heard a voice above him.

"Introducing our next challenger, Zoltar the Venomari!"

Zoltar slid into the pit. He had green, shimmery scales with red markings, and long, white fangs. Kai shivered. If a Venomari spit venom into your eyes, it caused hallucinations. It had happened to Kai once, and everyone he saw looked like a gingerbread man or woman.

"Um, I just came here to see Big Dan!" Kai called out. "I'll be going now."

"Spin the wheel! Spin the wheel!" the crowd chanted.

A rickety wheel came down from the ceiling. A Serpentine gave it a spin, and it clicked around and around. Kai read the categories around the wheel: spikes, poison, water, nets. *Must be battle extras,* he thought. *Pretty serious stuff.*

"Honestly, I need to get home now," Kai said. But the two Constrictai blocked his way. Then the wheel came to a stop.

"It's fire!" the announcer blared.

Kai paused. "Fire?"

What would be the harm in one more round? This time he'd be battling a Serpentine bad guy. Way more his speed. After all, battling bad guys was what ninja did — as a team or solo.

Is it really? a tiny voice asked in the back of his mind. *Is this what it means to be a ninja? Is this what Zane would have wanted?*

Kai shook the thought away. At least he'd get to use his **fire powers**!

"What is your name, Challenger?" the announcer asked Kai.

Kai grinned. "Just call me ... the Red Shogun!"

Chapter 11

Son, you are watching too much television," Sensei Garmadon scolded Lloyd.

"I've only been watching for a couple of hours," Lloyd complained.

"It's been four and a half hours exactly," his father corrected him. "You're supposed to be helping Cyrus Borg test his holographic system tomorrow. Shouldn't you be training?"

"Yeah, I guess," Lloyd said without much energy. Cyrus was expecting the whole ninja team. But Lloyd hadn't seen or heard from them in weeks. He was starting to wonder if he would ever see them again, and that made him sad.

"Come on, meet me in the training room," Garmadon said. "It will be fun."

Lloyd sighed and stretched. "Okay, Dad." He reached for the remote — and then stopped.

There, on his TV screen, was Jay! He was wearing a glittery blue suit and holding a microphone.

Sensei Garmadon stared. "Is he wearing . . . makeup?"

"I'm Jay, Ninjago's most lovable ninja!" Jay announced. "And I'm here before the Gauntlet of Humility to see who will be Ninjago's next hero . . . and whose dreams will be gone in a flash!"

"No way!" Lloyd cried. "He's a **game show host**!"

Lloyd felt a surge of energy. "Come on, Dad, let's go," he said, jumping off the couch.

He knew where to find Jay! That was a start. And if he could find Jay, that meant he could find the others, too. He may not get the team back together in time for Cyrus Borg's test, but he was going to get the team back together.

"Or I'm not the Green Ninja!" Lloyd said out loud.

"Yes, you are the Green Ninja," said Sensei Garmadon. "I knew that."

Lloyd blushed. "Sorry, just thinking out loud," he said. "Dad, I've got a new mission!"

"As long as it doesn't involve watching hours of television on end, I will support you," said his father.

Lloyd knew he could find Jay at the television station. That left Kai and Cole.

To find Kai, he went to see Nya at Sensei Wu's Academy.

"I haven't seen Kai in weeks," Nya told him. "I'm a little worried. But I did hear this rumor recently."

"Rumor?" Lloyd asked.

"There's a place called Yang Tavern, downtown. Guys who want to show off their fighting skills go there and compete in a Slither Pit. Bad guys mostly. Except . . ." Her voice trailed off. "There's a new guy in the pit. He calls himself the **Red Shogun**. And they say he can control fire."

Lloyd's eyes got wide. "That's Kai! It's got to be!"

Nya nodded. "That's what I think. I told him he needed to cool off, but I guess he didn't take my advice."

"I guess not," agreed Lloyd. "Thanks, Nya."

Finding out where Cole had gone was the most difficult. Lloyd searched the whole city, but nobody had seen him. Finally, he borrowed a hound dog and had it sniff one of Cole's old socks.

"Can you find Cole?" Lloyd asked.

The dog took off like a shot, pulling Lloyd behind him. He led Lloyd outside of the city, across a big field, and into the woods.

"Blackwood Forest," Lloyd said. He could smell the damp earth in the air. Of course Cole would come here. It made sense!

Lloyd knew what he had to do now. One by one, he would approach his friends. And one by one, he would ask them this simple request: Meet me at Master Chen's Noodle House. Let's talk.

Would the ninja be willing to listen to him? Would they want to be a team again?

Lloyd wasn't sure. But strangely, he wasn't worried. Seeing Jay and finding out where the others were had given him a feeling he hadn't had in weeks — hope.

The others missed the team as much as he did. He was sure of it.

They'll come, Lloyd told himself. *I know they will. We will be a team once again!*